I'm Your Bus

by
Marilyn Singer

pictures by
Evan Polenghi

SCHOLASTIC INC.
New York Toronto London Auckland
Sydney Mexico City New Delhi Hong Kong

Many thanks to my fabulous editor, Andrea Davis Pinkney, and the swell folks at Scholastic, and to my always-helpful husband, Steve Aronson. —M.S.

Special thanks to Andrea Davis Pinkney and Marijka Kostiw for driving this bus with grace and style. And an extra-special *beep* of gratitude to Barbara Greenberg for bringing all of us together. —E.P.

ISBN-13: 978-0-545-08919-7
ISBN-10: 0-545-08919-0

12 11 10 9 8 7 6 5 4 3 2 1   9 10 11 12 13 14/0

Printed in the U.S.A.   08

This edition first printing, September 2009

The text type was set in Gill Sans Bold.
The display type was set in F 2 F Tagliatelle Sugo, and Chancy DeluxxeBold.
The illustrations in this book were done in digital media.
Book design by Marijka Kostiw

To Andrew and Mary —M.S.

To my nephews,

Ethan & Julian Quinn —E.P.

Howdy, you can count on us.

Morning, evening, I'm your bus.

Sweepers sweeping, bakers baking.

Dawn is barely even breaking.

Time for buses to be waking!

Hurry, hurry, now it's eight!

Busy buses can't be late.

In the morning we won't wait!

Get on, Jamie, Carlos, Gus,

Casey, Lacey. I'm your bus.

Past the waving traffic cop.

Past the friendly tire shop.

There's the school zone.

Buses, stop!

Watch those backpacks coming through.

Have fun today. Learn something new.

Later we'll come back for you.

Hailey, Michael, Hannah, Russ,

see you later. I'm your bus.

On the seats, we buses find

lots of schoolbooks—every kind—

pencils, glasses left behind.

Bats and caps—how fabulous!

I'll keep them safe 'cause I'm your bus.

Buses may take you to see

a zoo, a farm, a factory.

We linger outside patiently.

Taxis zip by on their way
to an airport or café.
Buses go home, sit, and stay.

Quiet hours, we don't fuss.
Parking, driving, I'm your bus.

Yay! The school day's at an end.

Kids are leaving. They depend on each bus to be a friend.

Buses lined up in a row.

Lisa, Devin, Chloe, Mo,

find your bus and off you'll go!

How'd you grade me? Wow, A+!

I'm so proud that I'm your bus.

Night is falling. Watchmen guard.

Buses settled in the yard.

We had fun and we worked hard.

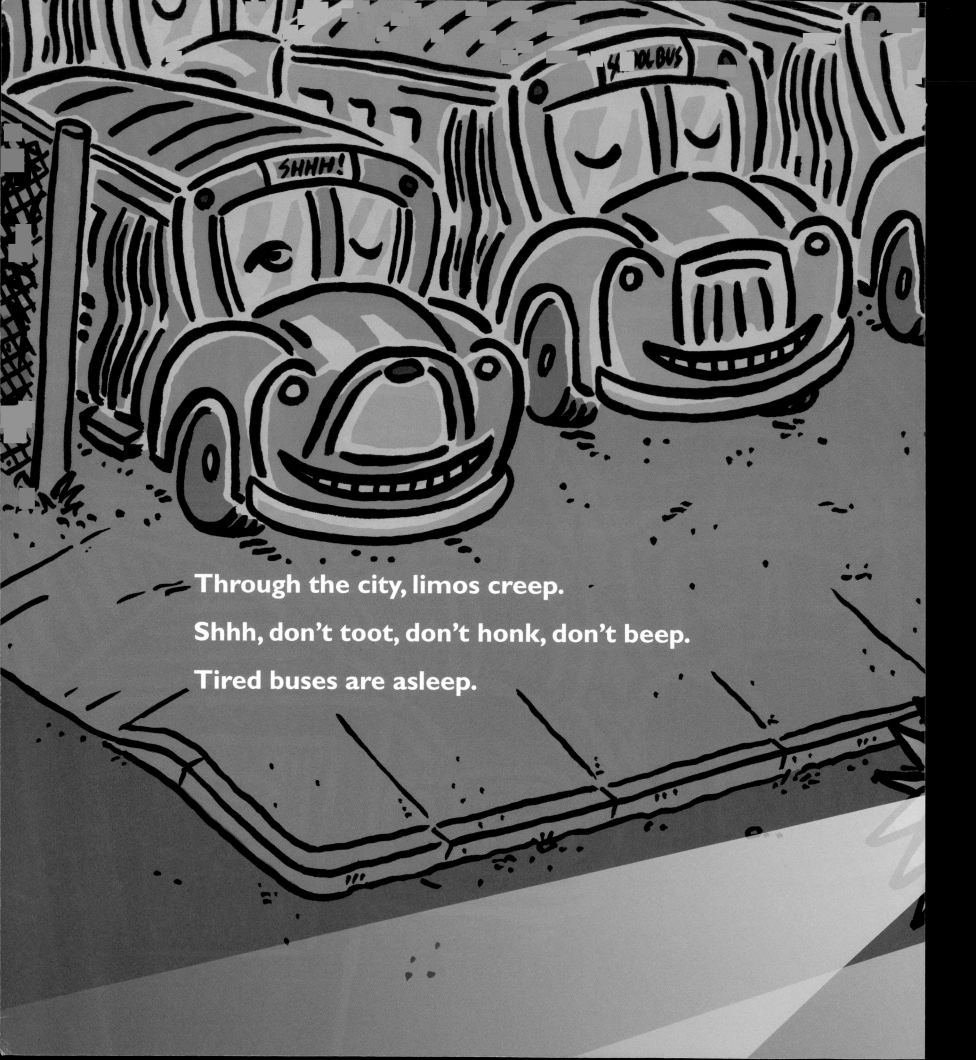

Through the city, limos creep.

Shhh, don't toot, don't honk, don't beep.

Tired buses are asleep.

Tomorrow you can count on us.

Daytime, nighttime, I'm your bus.